Sabelina: Sorceress Spy
Part 2: The Death of Innocence

Manuel Ortega Abis

Ukiyoto Publishing

All global publishing rights are held by

Ukiyoto Publishing

Published in 2022

Content Copyright © Manuel Ortega Abis

ISBN 9789360165413

All rights reserved.
No part of this publication may be reproduced, transmitted, or stored in a retrieval system, in any form by any means, electronic, mechanical, photocopying, recording or otherwise, without the prior permission of the publisher.

The moral rights of the author have been asserted.

This is a work of fiction. Names, characters, businesses, places, events, locales, and incidents are either the products of the author's imagination or used in a fictitious manner. Any resemblance to actual persons, living or dead, or actual events is purely coincidental.

This book is sold subject to the condition that it shall not by way of trade or otherwise, be lent, resold, hired out or otherwise circulated, without the publisher's prior consent, in any form of binding or cover other than that in which it is published.

www.ukiyoto.com

*This is the death of innocence
of Isabela Manlavi
as she embarked on her spellbinding missions
as Sabelina, the first Filipino sorceress spy.*

CONTENTS

Black Moon's Eve	1
Skin-Deep	6
The First Cut Is The Deepest	11
Escape To The Hills	15
Propinquities	20
Takeover	24
Unknown	28
Succubus Mode Unlocked	32
Daughter, Behold Thy Father	36
Tenebris Manus	40
Happy Birthday, Isabela	44
Perplexions	48
Épilogue Temporaire	52
About the Author	*54*

Black Moon's Eve

"It is going to be awhile. I will need to take the long way home. It is hard to explain."

- Abismo

*

Seven days before Isabela Manlavi's 18th birthday.

It was already almost two hours before midnight, but Sebastian "Basti" Gomez still could not sleep. For a year, he had been staying in the ancestral home of his father's family in Quezon City.

He had just finished talking with his uncle, Father Roberto Aquino, who expressed his own excitement to their impending reunion set as a surprise on Isabela's 18th birthday.

Little did the two realize that the young woman had been ambushed by an unknown assailant or assailants while she and her supposed BFF, or best friend forever, Claire, were on their way to a baylian in the aplaya south of the town of Pantalan.

"Yes, Papito! I would bring the Serc capsules you need for your vertigo." Basti called Father Roberto as Father Tito, or Papito, as a sort of portmanteau of the priest being his uncle and his second father. Ever since the death of his real father, Fredo, Basti saw Father Roberto as his surrogate parent. Thus, Papito, the combination of the words Papa and Tito.

"Thank you, my son," the priest replied with a full smile over the web camera of his laptop. "By the way, your sister Isabela had been pestering me for over a week now. Asking me if you knew about her birthday next week. I made up some excuse. Just enough to make her think that you're a 'maybe' when it comes to attending her birthday. I think she bought it."

Basti could not refrain himself. "Oh, Papito, I wouldn't miss it for the world! I arranged for a flight on the morning of her birthday, so that by the afternoon I would already be there. I have also gift-wrapped our birthday gift for her. The six instruments of the Kublis!"

Father Roberto's eyes glowed with delight. Suddenly, however, he remembered something. Basti noticed the priest's change of demeanor on the monitor of his laptop.

"What's the matter, Papito?"

"Nothing, my son. Well, to tell you the truth, I really wanted one more thing as a birthday gift for our Isabela. The one thing that she was with when I first saw her that stormy December night on the chapel steps."

Basti understood.

Father Roberto was referring to none other than the Spiritus Lucis Deo necklace that his daughter somehow lost the first time she entered the Black Mirror inside the Ossuarium.

"Anyway," the good priest felt guilty of dampening the mood of Basti, "aside from our gift, I'm sure Isabela would be more than excited to know that you've been promoted once more!"

"Yes, Papito! As an NBI Head Agent! Just a rank lower of being an Assistant Director! At first I wasn't sure if I'd get it. You know these things, Papito. The politics. The padrino system…"

"Yes, yes, I understand. I guess your Lolo Vito and Father Guido - as well as your Tatay - are still using their influences in Heaven in our favor! Hahaha!"

Basti also laughed with a small tinge of sadness. "Hahaha! I guess so, Papito…"

*

How many times Basti had turned over and over in his bed, the young man could no longer count. More than a dozen years older than Isabela, the eldest son of Fredo and the youngest member of their covert guild, the Shafts of Light, wrestled with so many questions that had only been clear to him these past few years.

One of the main questions swirling inside his brain right now was: What is going to be my role in our mission?

The other questions were merely offshoots of the primary: While my role is not even that clear to me yet, how could Father Roberto decide without any doubt that Isabela's the chosen one? Why her - and why not me?

To Basti, if there ever was a person in the country right now who would be able to succeed and who be able to combine wizardry and the skills and talent as a spy, it would definitely be him.

In a way, the things running in his head made him feel that maybe the three other senior members of the Shafts of Light - his lolo, Father Guido, and now his Papito - had been holding something out from him. Keeping him in the dark. And maybe even from his father when Fredo was still alive.

Basti suddenly felt a surge of anger, not caring whether it was justified or not, when he recalled the circumstances of his own father's passing.

Wilfredo died inside the subterranean caverns of the kegelkarst of Batigong. Lolo Vito told Basti it was an accident. But he could not believe his great grandfather's explanation. Fredo had confessed to him earlier that, while he was assessing the caves, he had had numerous encounters with the otherworldly; and that these encounters were not for the faint of heart. Fredo believed the tenebris manus, the hands of darkness, of the Black Moon were behind these attacks against him inside the caverns. Alas, when Fredo reported these to the Shafts of Light during one of their regular monthly meetings then, the majority dismissed it as unfounded, and that Fredo instead should focus his energy and attention to accomplishing his tasks.

"Why did they not believe my father? Was it because he was only considered a colgante, or in Filipino a sampid, of the family? If they so thought of his father this way, why did they make him a member of the Shafts of Light in the first place?"

Finally, Basti sat up from his bed. He sought to purge himself with all the negative thoughts and emotions which had somehow built up inside him. He believed that, for his part, his task to be prepared for the next phase of their mission he had already accomplished well beyond what was expected of him. His target was merely to be a full-fledged agent so he could be in the position to help from inside the NBI. And now that he became a head agent, he was now in a much better position.

"Oh, sorry, my Papito, my Isabela, if these thoughts and emotions are still haunting me these past few years! But I believe that when we finally meet face-to-face, all the negativity and doubts I have been beset with these past few weeks will pass!"

Instead of going back to bed, Basti took to texting someone on his phone. Someone he knew would be able to appease his long-buried emotions.

Serena.

*

More or less an hour before midnight.

The young, well-endowed head of the criminal syndicate White Ant Queen, Lei Versoza, shoved one side of her bosom on the shoulder of the older but brutally handsome King Carlos of the nefarious Exilium Rex Corporation. King Carlos, or KC to those who knew him well, turned his head to Lei.

Lei whispered to KC, "Couldn't stand this shit anymore. Let's go back to the room they gave me upstairs. I'll show you a much better ceremony than this fucking shit."

In the shadows, the two made their way out of the large suite where the Black Moon's new leader, Mangbubuhok, was about to start a darker version of a Palawan babaylan ritual called the Lambayan, a purification ceremony.

Mangbubuhok, a bayok, the feminized son of the babaylan Antegena, and now the appointed leader of their occultist crime group, the Black Moon, had his eyes closed, but he could sense, using his third eye, that two of his guests, Lei and KC, exited the suite during the particular occasion that was supposed to be the most important cycle of his criminal group's Klaraws. The Klaraws could be described as the clearly defined seasons in the life of deities, as well as their appointed human intermediaries, such as babaylans. These eight seasons included the Lambayan. But while the real Lambayan ceremony by Palawan babaylans was a purification ceremony meant to purify the spirit of the dead so that its way to nowhere elseness would not be hampered, the Black Moon's version of this ritual was more horrific. It involved a feast, then an orgy, and then finally culminating with a human sacrifice at the moment the prophesied black moon eclipse would become visible in the heavens.

"You are all invited here tonight to witness the rise of the Truth from the darkness we have all thrived in!" Mangbubuhok's voice echoed on the four corners of the large suite. "Bring in the virgin sacrifice!"

Two burly and sinister-looking Black Moon cohorts brought in the sacrifice before Mangbubuhok who stood before a long table that was turned into an altar of sort.

The so-called virgin sacrifice was wearing a black hood over its head. And when one of the men who escorted it finally took the hood off, Mangbubuhok saw the fearful eyes of Isabela's BFF, Claire. The young woman who, for some unknown reason, was foiled in trying to stab Isabela on their way to a baylian four hours earlier.

Skin-Deep

"The truth will set you free, but first it will make you miserable."

- Father Guido Arguelles

*

Half an hour before midnight.

For the record, the last five years or so had already shed most of Nanay Leni's fat down the drain. After a strict regimen of exercise and diet, the woman had transformed into a physical form that was more to her own liking rather than to anybody else's. What inspired her most was not really the mariteses of the town of Pantalan who kept harping on the woman's lack of exercise as well as dietary discipline. What inspired her most was the fact that the "incident" in the church of Pantalan nine years ago became a blessing in disguise for her, with her former suitor, then Col. Segundo Miraflores, revealing to her the Tagbanua lineage of Father Roberto; which, in turn, gave her the necessary leverage to make her sexual advances to the priest more pronounced as ever.

So when she decided to walk outside of her room again with only a flimsy nighties, without any underclothes on, she knew tonight would be a long and hard embattled one.

"I told them to be home by 10. What time did they leave, Father?" Nanay Leni asked, pretending that she did not notice the wide eyes of the man of God deeply probing her now.

"Ah, uhrm, around 8, I think."

"Oh, I missed the old days. Everybody in bed by 6. Just the radio coddling everybody to sleep. Remember how we used to listen to 'Mga Mata ni Anghelita'? You did remind the girls to bring flashlights?"

"Ah, yes, Nay, I mean, yes, of course, Leni. I did." The priest sighed with relief about the prospect of enjoying one evening without any unscheduled power outage. Black-outs were already being a part of their town's nostalgia for decades. Foreign tourists found out the hard way that a rural town without electricity running through its homes and streets had somehow turned the place into something more attuned to the country life they came - and paid handsomely - to expect. No electricity, no running water, no signal. Far from the city life these foreign tourists had become so adverse to.

The baylian in the aplaya, which was even out of the way of any dirt road or mud path, at the outskirts of the one of the remotest barrios of their island, and a power outage; the very thought of these things certainly incited something in the usually law-abiding brain of Nanay Leni, or now just Leni to Father Roberto, to mandate a grossly inhumane curfew for the two restless young ladies and for their raging hormones.

But who was she to be so strict to these young and restless souls searching for a way to celebrate their youth the only way they knew and understood how?

Indeed, if it was up to Leni, the good housekeeper that she was, would see to it that everybody in the good priest's home would be doing it the same way she and her family had been doing it in Pantalan: the last meal of the day at 5 p.m., and everybody in bed by 6 p.m.

But if only Leni fully understood: time and youth had their own way of trying to reinvent each other; trying to rediscover what were once not there, so that the known would give way to more unknowns, to more secrets, to more mysteries. And time would always have the upper hand against youth; making sure that before it was over, youth would be confessing everything. With or without the interrogation or the torture of anybody who would not want to be an agent of change.

In his youth, however, even Father Roberto was called just as such a change advocate. And more.

The priest opened his handy bible without reading it all, then slouched on his rattan butaka, crossing his legs but trying to keep them lower than his stomach.

Leni turned around to face the priest.

"Roberto…" Leni chose to address the priest now without the perfunctory title.

The man raised his head and asked the woman. "What is it, Leni?"

"It's almost midnight. Should I turn the hot water for the shower now?"

"Oh, sure, sure, Leni."

"But," the woman walked over to the priest and knelt before him, "I just would like to find out something."

"What?" Father Roberto nervously inquired.

"Roberto," Leni grabbed something between the man's thighs that was currently hidden by the open bible, "what is this? Can I take a look at it?"

*

A rat that had wandered aimlessly into the cold, damp, and misty underground chamber somewhere in the mountains of the island was able to find its way through it via a maze of crevices and corners, searching for something it could sink its teeth into. At last, it settled itself on an object hanging somewhat precariously in the air that appeared lifeless for the moment. But, to the rodent, was currently good enough to nibble on. The object was none other than the toe nail of the creature whose hands and torso were manacled tight and left dangling like a piece of smoked meat on the dimly-lit wall of a cavernous chamber. The rat leaped and caught the lifeless toe nail on its first try. But just as it was to nibble on it, it began to twitch back to life.

The creature hanging on the cave wall was none other than Isabela, the part of her skull where she was bludgeoned by a blunt object already numb, yet bleeding.

Dangling on the thick abacca ropes with her head bowed, the young woman started to feel the aches of her joints. As Isabela sought to open her eyes behind the disheveled bangs of her hair, she felt the pores of her flesh slowly processing the trauma that her body had experienced four hours earlier.

Still adjusting her senses to the sights and sounds of her new environment, the young woman tried to wriggle out of the ropes that bound her hands. She tried over and over and over, but to no avail. She was on the verge of desperation and was about to burst into tears coupled with a lung-draining yell, when something suddenly happened.

She had never felt such state of calm and clarity before.

Isabela started to take one slow and deep breath. Then another after that. Then another.

The young woman started to recall the breathing exercises her foster father, Father Roberto, trained her when she was still a girl of ten.

"That breath of air, my child, is your spiritus lucis. Your breath of light. Your spiritus lucis will keep your heart beating and your heart running; but it will be up to you, Isabela, on how you would keep yourself alive once your spiritus lucis has dissipated and starts to momentarily recharge."

No longer wasting any time, she heaved one more breath and concentrated. Though limited in its own powers, the spiritus lucis did have supernatural effects to the behavior of certain creatures and objects.

Once, Isabela taught herself to use her spiritus lucis to command a regiment of hantiks, or weaver ants, to dance on top of a matchbox. But now, beyond the dancing of red ants on a matchbox, the young woman had a crazy idea. So crazy that it might just work.

She closed her eyes and focused her full attention on the many crevices and corners of the cold, damp cavern.

"This had to work! Had to…"

Seconds turned into minutes, but nothing was happening.

Almost to the point of complete exhaustion, her brain working overtime, her heart beating wildly beyond it muscle, mold, and mass, Isabela opened her eyes. Then, one by one, she caught a glimpse of hope peering inside the crevices and behind the corners.

In fact, not just a glimpse, but an entire platoon of it.

Before Isabela could even blink her weary eyes, rats started swarming around her. Then the rodents started climbing up her body any which way they could. A couple of them managed to hang on to the slippery slope of her nose and hopped onto the bangs of her hair, then up her arms, and finally, their destination: the abacca ropes that bound Isabela's numbed wrists. Before the young woman could raise her head and try to look at her rescuers, the rats were gaining momentum, nibbling, nibbling, nibbling away at the ropes.

Moments later, the ropes gave in, and Isabela fell on the sodden ground with a loud thud.

With her brain still in the process of what to do next, the young apprentice sorceress waved one hand in the air to gesture her great gratitude to the creatures that had now made, in no uncertain terms, a lifelong bond with her.

"Thank you, guyz! I'll find a way to make it up to you, somehow, some way! But, right now, I have to find my way out of here!"

The First Cut Is The Deepest

"If you treat an individual as he is, he will remain how he is. But if you treat him as if he were what he ought to be and could be, he will become what he ought to be and could be."

- Johann Wolfgang von Goethe

*

Serena was a night person who plied her trade in the streets of Cubao's night joints.

When Basti first met Serena, the young woman was part of those arrested in a raid of a sex den owned by a powerful politician. Leading a lifestyle of no saintess, Serena was deep into sex, drugs, and alcohol before Basti reached out to her to help her climb out of the pit she was starting to bury herself into.

This part of her past was now behind her. After she knocked on the door of the apartment where Basti was staying, and after the door opened, Serena understood that it was up to her take that step over a threshold where the dark fragments of her past could no longer pose a danger.

"Hi, Basti, it's close to midnight and still couldn't sleep?"

The newly-promoted NBI head agent smiled sheepishly at Serena.

"Well, you know how the saying goes: if you can't beat 'em, join 'em."

"Oh, now you're making me guilty of my taking the job as a CSR in UP-Technohub. You're in luck because it's my off tonight."

"Now that's the best news I've heard… uh, uh, urghhh…"

"Basti! Basti! What's happening?"

The young man fell on the floor of his apartment like a log and started convulsing and writhing violently.

"Basti! Basti! What's happening to you, love?"

*

A few seconds after the stroke of midnight, after Mangbubuhok pierced the talim, or the magic dagger, into the heart of Claire as the virgin sacrifice, the leader of the Black Moon declared to all who were present in his large suite that, "The time has finally come for the reckoning of their world!"

A few floors up, however, two of Black Moon's guests laid in bed, twisted together in a love knot that neither of the two would prefer to untie for the moment.

Lei, the woman who preferred to sit up on the bed, exposing her well-hung breasts areolas, nipples, and all, suddenly asked KC as she lit up a stick of cigarette and blew a puff of smoke in the air, "So you're telling me that poor, young woman down there, that wasn't the one referred to in the so-called Masirikampu prophecies?"

KC groaned with his answer behind a pillow he placed over his head. It was more of a comic-sounding watered down snore rather than a groan.

"So, hey! I hope you're listening, okay? So, what's the point of the whole sacrifice shebang down there? Just to show to us what?"

"Quit griping and go back to bed."

Lei blew another puff of smoke and placed the cigarette on the ashtray beside a small lamp on the night stand.

"If you ask me there are only two kinds of magic I believe in this world: money…"

The young woman started to fondle KC's limp cock.

"… and this!"

*

Still a bit woozy from her traumatic experience, the daughter of Father Roberto who had been secretly undergoing physical and spiritual training as an apprentice sorceress for almost a decade already started to weave her way in the dimly-lit maze of the cavernous chamber she had been thrown into and brutally restrained by a force of yet unknown origin. Foremost in her mind was: Who bludgeoned her? She tried to feel the gaping wound on her skull. While it had already dried out and closed up a bit, the pain still made the young woman wince her eyes as she struggled to crawl her way out of her current predicament.

Her rescuers, her furry, little friends, appeared to have one more mission in their minds. They rats seemed to act as her escorts as she lumbered along the natural corridors of the cave. Apparently not only as escorts, but seemingly as guides. They waddled and hopped in front of the apprentice sorceress who had successfully used the training she got from her foster father.

Her spiritus lucis.

She remembered the necklace Father Roberto gave her as a graduation gift almost ten years ago.

Little did Isabela realized that that special necklace had been hers from the beginning. For, when she was delivered on the chapel door of Pantalan by her still unrevealed deliverers to this world eighteen years ago, that special necklace bearing the inscription "Spiritus Lucis Deo" on its backside was duly kept by Father Roberto; knowing that he would be giving it to her, sooner or later, and for whatever purpose it may serve in her life.

Suddenly, the rats that were acting as escorts to Isabela stopped in their tracks. Her furry, little rescuers started to sniff around. They appeared to be talking to each other. Even the young apprentice sorceress seemed to be understanding what the rats were saying to each other. That there was imminent danger ahead of them. Or, more specifically, hanging around the ceiling of the cavernous chamber; hovering above them. Waiting to pounce on them.

Before Isabela could even react. The rats fanned out and each and every one of them began to make its way to the nearest crevice and began to turn the nearest corner of the cave. In an instant, her furry, little friends disappeared before her eyes. But not before the bats descended on some of the slower moving ones, the ones that panicked and shrieked instead of moving their butts to the nearest escape hatch.

Isabela was swarmed by the bats, but they did not harm a strand of hair on her. The young woman closed her eyes and concentrated as the bats hovered and shrieked wildly around her with some of them perched on the walls of chamber, clawing their way into the crevices where the young woman's rescuers hid themselves.

Fully recharged, Isabela again used her spiritus lucis. She heaved one deep breath. Then another. Then another.

When the young woman opened her eyes again, the bats had already flown back to the ceiling of the cave; seemingly awaiting her next instructions to them.

And as all these transpired rather in quick and expedient fashion, Isabela heard a voice from a glimmer of light that suddenly appeared before her.

"Welcome home, my child!"

Escape To The Hills

"They who dream by day are cognizant of many things which escape those who dream only by night."

- Edgar Allan Poe

*

The flashlight of a cellphone lit up from the edge of a ricefield paddy, a few meters from the foot of the mountains arrayed on the northeastern side of the island. Three shadows huddled around it.

"Ka Iboy, the soldiers had already put up checkpoints on both the northern and southern borders of the Pantalan main road going in and out of the town. The distraction I've created near the marketplace should give us a bit more time. But it won't take long before they decide to comb the mountains for us."

The young man called Ka Iboy nodded his head as he rested one hand on the neck of his long firearm. After a pause of a few seconds, the young man spoke.

"We'll go to the lake at the foot of the hill. They won't be able to follow us there until the sun rises about four, five hours from now. Old man," Ka Iboy addressed the third person in the huddle who had been quietly sitting and listening to the two, "it's already 1am. Let's not have Maring worry about where you are. Don't worry. The soldiers won't even suspect of any involvement from you. Don Simeon's crimes are against the people. Burning his kamalig is just part of the committee's sentence on him. So, go home, Ka Ramon…"

Hardly had Ka Iboy's words left his lips when a violent hail of bullets rained a few feet from where they were huddled. A glaring searchlight was then switched on from somewhere on the paddies.

The three hurriedly broke up the huddle as flashes of light and another round of blazing gunfire ensued once more.

"Mang Ramon! Quick! Here!" As Ka Iboy started to move further deep into the shadows, he was too late to notice that his two companions had already taken hits: one took a bullet right between his eyes, and the old man he called as Mang Ramon was hit right on his left leg.

"Mang Ramon!" Ka Iboy turned just in time to watch the old man sprawled on the ground with a pistol ready to fire in his hand. Mang Ramon grimaced in pain, but managed to gesture for him to get on with his own escape.

Having second thoughts of leaving the old man, nonetheless Ka Iboy immediately decided to obey the voice of experience.

In the darkness of that fatal hour after midnight and unbeknownst to a rebel whose heart and mind were racing through the dense forest of a mountain going up the ridge leading to Batigong hill, the reign of the Black Moon had just begun.

*

"Roberto! What's the matter?"

"Uh, I don't know, Len," the priest uttered in pain as he rolled off the bed and fell down on the floor.

The two illicit lovers were in the throes of wild ecstasy when Father Roberto felt something on his chest.

Leni initially thought it was some sort of myocardial infarction, a heart attack. But when her Roberto rose from the floor and started pounding his own chest with his bare knuckles, the woman understood that it was different from a mere heart attack.

"I, uh, I, uh, Len… I feel like… I have been stabbed in my heart by something sharp… by a dagger…"

Len quickly wrapped the blanket around her naked body and got up from the bed. So many things were running in her head. It would be the most grave scandal of the town of Pantalan if it would be discovered that Father Roberto died on the bed of his manang friday.

"Oh, please, dear Lord! Not my Roberto..." Leni already had her arms around the priest's head.

The pain appeared to have subsided, but Father Roberto still had his eyes closed. He was breathing heavily from both his nose and his mouth.

"Are you alright, Roberto? How do you feel right now?"

The priest did not answer.

How could Father Roberto offer a reply to a question he himself had no inkling whatsoever on what just occurred to his own person?

*

Mangbubuhok showed the talim, the magic dagger, to his right hand man, the notoriously famous hitman, Sergei.

As the leader of the occultist criminal syndicate Black Moon did so, Mangbubuhok then recited a verse from the mysterious Masirikampu prophecies:

"A touch of mirror wherever, whenever,

A touch of mirror that cuts through space and time;

A drop of blood shall bind forever

All, without exceptions, all our adversaries and its entire clan."

Though still a bit skeptical, Sergei, nodded his head and studied the unique shape of the talim's handle and blade.

"And you're telling me that that ritual you did before us earlier? That should have been the final nail on those who want to erase the Black Moon from the face of the earth?"

"Yes, my child! The death of all our enemies! Death to each and every one of them! Just you wait and see! Just you wait and see, my child!"

*

During the full moon that passed an hour earlier at the stroke of midnight, and from a distinct vantage point, the Black Moon towers, built on an undisclosed location just outside the National Capital

Region, created a silhouette that resembled an intricately designed cup.

To the babaylans of Pantalan in the rothern region of Palawan, the cup as described was the kalis.

Babaylans used the kalis merely as a vessel to carry the drink that was imbibed during the many rituals of their Klaraws.

To the Black Moon leader, however, Mangbubuhok used the kalis as a dripping pan for the blood of their exsanguinated human sacrifices.

The NBI investigators who first found out about the existence of the Black Moon at first dismissed the group as another one of those small cult groups that was destined to self-destruct. Most of these cult groups centered around the personality of their leader; and once the head was cut off, so to speak, the entire body perished with it.

As the heir apparent of Antegena, the founder of Black Moon, Mangbubuhok was well aware of this suicidal tendency of the organization. That was the reason why he made it sure he was one step ahead of all those who wanted the organization outed from the criminal underworld scene as soon as possible.

Unfortunately, this was not to be, however. Mangbubuhok soon found out that he did not only inherit a criminal would-be empire, but an entirely different world of the supernatural where he - as a babaylan - possessed all the power he needed to accumulate more power, more wealth, and, more significantly, more knowledge on how to use that power and that wealth to make the whole world kneel before him.

In fact, at the same time when the NBI imported the KHULAM machine as part of its covert Spiyamahika program in Pantalan, the Black Moon had just purchased in the black market a hybrid version of the machine for half the price but twice the collateral damage.

In short, Mangbubuhok prepared the Black Moon for something bigger than merely being a criminal organization based in the Philippines. His confidence did not rely on sheer luck, of course. He had a secret weapon far more deadlier than the hybrid KHULAM machine he had bought for the group. A secret, living, and breathing weapon that neither the NBI nor the remnants of the Shafts of Light would not have expected to be on the black side of the moon at all.

Propinquities

"To understand just one life you have to swallow the world ... do you wonder, then, that I was a heavy child?"

– Salman Rushdie, Midnight's Children

*

"Welcome home, Isabela. Have you come to finally claim your throne?"

The voice was somehow disturbingly familiar to Isabela.

"Who are you? Where am I? Why did you hurt me?"

"We were not the ones who hurt you, Isabela! It was the tenebris manus of the Black Moon that attacked you! They even used Claire to get to you! We were the ones who rescued you from them!"

Upon hearing the name of her BFF, Isabela's senses returned to their keenness.

"What happened to Claire? Where is she?"

Silence.

"Why don't you answer me? Where is...?"

"Claire is gone, Isabela."

The young apprentice sorceress fell on her knees and started to weep profusely.

"What happened to her?" Isabela asked the question more to herself than to the mysterious voice inside the cave.

"She was possessed by Mangbubuhok, Isabela."

The words of the voice did not really register in the young woman's mind for the moment.

"What happened to Claire...?" Isabela repeated.

"Isabela, Isabela. Please listen to me. Do you want to save Claire's soul?"

The young woman covered her face with her hands. She had never felt so powerless in her life.

"Isabela, please open your eyes. You can save Claire's soul - with this!"

A mysterious glow of light suddenly appearing hovering in front of Isabela. The young woman felt the warmth coming from the glow that was slowly growing stronger and stronger. She opened her eyes and saw a holographic image of the part of her past she thought she had lost forever: the Spiritus Lucis Deo necklace!

"My necklace!"

"Yes, Isabela! This is your inheritance as heir to the throne of the realm of the Black Mirror! I ask you once more, my child: Have you come to finally claim back your throne, oh, Queen?"

Throwing all her caution, and even her own sanity, aside, Isabela stood up and with an unexpected resolute tone in her voice answered, "Yes, I, Isabela Manlavi, hereby claim my throne as your Queen!"

Suddenly, the entire cave glowed as bright as a thousand suns. In less than one blink of an eye, Isabela was transported back to her bed in 21 Calle Baragatan, deep in her sleep, and finally wearing around her neck the omnipotence of the Spiritus Lucis Deo.

*

The next morning, Father Roberto and Basti conversed over the phone to talk about the experiences they both had which were oddly similar in many respects.

"So, Papito, you also felt that sort of being stabbed in your heart?"

"Yes, my son! I did recover after an hour or so. Nanay Leni was so worried she was about to call the hospital…"

"Same here, Papito. Good thing that Serena was with me."

"Serena? How about…?"

"No! No, Papito, she, she wasn't here. And any line of communication we had for almost ten years now was all but broken."

Father Roberto paused for a few seconds before continuing.

"Anyway, I did do some research when I woke up an hour ago. I read some verses from the Masirikampu prophecies. I emailed them to you earlier. There are 2 sets: the one that pertained to Isabela's 18th birthday, and the one that, I think, is directly related to us."

Basti quickly opened up his email account and checked the verses his uncle had sent him.

"A touch of mirror wherever, whenever,

A touch of mirror that cuts through space and time;

A drop of blood shall bind forever

All, without exceptions, all our adversaries and its entire clan."

Basti's chin fell.

"Papito, you don't think...?"

"I would like to think otherwise, my son. But if there was one lesson that last night's experience clearly showed us: we are all in this together."

*

After their conversation over the phone, Basti got up from the chair and returned to his bedroom.

Serena was still in bed asleep.

The young man knelt on the floor near the foot of the bed and quietly took out a large paper bag. He then tiptoed back outside to inspect the content of the bag.

Already giftwrapped, Basti tore without hesitation the box that he got out of the paper bag. He opened the box and checked out the contents. The six instruments of the Kublis. One by one he spread the half dozen objects on the floor of his apartment.

Basti was particularly interested in one of the objects. The so-called talim, or magical dagger. As he picked it up, he remembered what his

Tatay Fredo once told him about the Kublis, and how its instruments could be used as weapons against their adversaries.

"Whatever is born from earth, we can use as a tool or as a weapon against our enemies. For they are also born of earth, whatever form or shape they may choose to take while fighting us. They are and will always be lamang-lupa! Creatures of the earth!"

"What's that, love?"

Basti immediately recognized the voice behind him, quickly collected the objects from the floor, and threw them all inside the paper bag.

"Oh, nothing! I just wasn't sure I bought the right gift for my sister in Palawan…"

"So," Serena's voice was a bit inquisitive, but not that intrusive so as to stir any argument, "you're really going to push through with your trip over there? Any chance I could come along with you?"

As Basti walked over to his sort of work table nearby he opened the lock of an overhead cabinet, placed the bag inside, then locked the cabinet again.

"Well, you see, dear, I haven't been in my hometown for more than two decades. I don't even have an idea on how they would treat me once I get there. You know what I mean, my father being merely a half-brother to my uncle there."

"A brother is still a brother, mahal. If you come to think of it, we are all interconnected one way or another." Just as Serena finished her last statement, she approached Basti and wrapped her arms around her lover's waist. "So what say you if you and me go back to bed and make some interconnections before we get some breakfast outside?"

Takeover

"I know nothing in the world that has as much power as a word. Sometimes I write one, and I look at it, until it begins to shine."

— Emily Dickinson

*

Either of the two must have been Atty. Magalona's plan all along: the abolition of the entire Spiyamahika program, or the absolute takeover of it.

As Dr. Sim read the wording of the memo coming from headquarters and signed by the NBI Director himself, he tried to assimilate in his brain not only the reasons, but the reasons behind the reasons for either of the two to be the mission of the lawyer who had started the internal auditing of the project he considered as his own baby.

While most of the employees might be inclined to cooperate with the lawyer, or else lose more than their jobs, Dr. Sim felt that among his peers there would one or two Judases who would not hesitate to betray his trust and confidence for less than thirty silver pieces.

He likened what he was thinking about to a father who had realized too late that he raised his child by sparing the rod, and now was ready to bite his pelvis.

"What should I do? I couldn't sit idly by and have this fucking lawyer mess up my life here in Spiyamahika! Ah, I know!"

Inside his office, Dr. Sim got out his cellphone and started dialing. The phone at the other end of the line rang only once before it was picked up.

"It's me. We have to meet. Today. I'll be there before noon."

*

Sunday arrived and left rather unassumingly in the town of Pantalan. Father Roberto did his usual sermons during the morning masses he presided, but for the evening masses he decided to turn over the Eucharist celebration to a lay minister who had neither the zeal nor the charisma of the parish priest of the church of Pantalan.

While the town had started reaping the benefits of having its main road interconnected from north to south of the island borders, the flurry of activities that were normally associated with the heavy influx of tourists and pilgrims, foreign and domestic, had not been present for the past few weeks.

Credit went, of course, to the rebels hiding in the mountainside who were sowing fear and terror among the Pantalanons these past few months. And although Gen. Segundo Miraflores swore that he would take down every last one of these "bastards" before the end of the year, well into the seventh month of the year, August, and the townsfolks of Pantalan felt no closer to the promise the army officer had made to them.

Discredit went, not so unexpectedly, to the local government of Pantalan which could not seem to get its act together in improving lives of its constituents as well as the services they promised to deliver to them. Foremost of these services was power. The rampant blackouts was a big headache to everybody. It was also being exploited by the rebels in the mountains as one of their campaigns to win the hearts and minds particularly of the youth in Pantalan who appeared to have resigned to the fact that their future would be better off fighting those in power rather than remaining subservient to them.

While the whole of Sunday might have come and gone rather unassumingly, Monday arrived with a bit of surprise for the residents of 21 Calle Baragatan.

"LBC po! Delivery!"

Nanay Leni could not help herself thinking that the package, whose dimensions were somewhat as big as a balikbayan box, contained a very special birthday gift for a very special someone.

"For Ms. Isabela Manlavi po!"

Her suspicions were steadily proving to be correct. A bit heavy to drag into the young woman's room, Nanay Leni told the messenger to bring it inside the house and set it beside the still locked door of Isabela's room.

When the LBC messenger left, Father Roberto's manang friday, and secret lover, was about to knock on the door when Isabela surprisingly came out of her room.

"Wow, anak! It must be some sort of furniture or something! Or are you expecting a balikbayan box from a friend, or someone special? Uuuy, my little girl's a grown up naaa! Haaay, your birthday's this Saturday and I can't wait for it, hija!"

Nanay Leni might have been the disciplinarian in Isabela's life, but there were times she just could not hide her maternal instincts to the child she considered to be her own daughter.

"Hahaha! Nay, I don't think this came from abroad! But I have to bring it inside my room! Later I'll tell you what it is! Later, Nay!"

With a frown in her face, Nanay Leni helped push the big box inside Isabela's room.

Once inside the room, the young woman locked the door and pulled the curtains down from the windows.

After her surreal experience two night ago, she developed supernatural instincts which she had not had before. And one of them was the power of premonition.

Isabela got a cutter from her night stand, knelt in front of the box, and started cutting open the heavily taped box.

Soon as she was satisfied with the cutting process, she placed the cutter down on the floor and started peeling the top side of the box open. Then she pulled out what looked like - one-half of a full body mirror whose glass was as black as a raven's wing.

Along with the mirror, she picked herself up from the floor and leaned the mysterious object on one wall of her room.

Right away, the supernatural happened.

The black mirror transformed into none other than Sefiro, Isabela's trainer in the realm of the Black Mirror.

"Hi, Sefiro! Welcome to my world!"

"Isabela, my child," spoke with an urgency that Isabela expected, "we have no time to waste! As agreed, the Goddess of Darkness would be communicating with you through your dreams. And I am now tasked with the mission of training you to be Our Royal Sorceress! Isabela, please listen well…"

Sefiro then told the young apprentice sorceress what was about to happen in the next few days. But the handsome trainer, who appeared to have not aged a day since they met almost a decade ago, made sure he got one thing straightened out in Isabela's mind.

"Isabela, my child, if you push through with your birthday celebration this Saturday, you would be putting yourself and your father in imminent danger!"

Unknown

"Secrets that make us invisible to the world are not as hurtful as those that make us invisible to ourselves."

- Abismo

*

Along with two other people inside his office, NBI Director Rodolfo Ricablanca watched on a television set the Special Report series by ATV News Net, currently the top Asian TV news network. It centered on Salamangka, supposedly the first spy satellite launched more than a month ago from Philippine soil.

The program had been swathed with intrigue when, last week, the Philippine national government's partner from the private sector for the special satellite program by the Dept. of National Defense, the CEO of Exilium Rex Corp., King Carlos, or KC, was alleged to have been heavily involved with a sex and drug ring leader who had known ties with the Hong Kong drug triad, a certain Lei Versoza of the White Ant Queen criminal syndicate.

The NBI Director listened intently to the special news report:

"The ATV News Net team tried to get Exilium Rex's as well as Miss Lei Versoza's side of the story, but to no avail. Meanwhile, in Malacañang, the President himself announced that the Salamangka spy satellite had been performing well beyond their expectations, and that, in the President's own words, "the country will be reaping the benefits from Salamangka very soon."

Further, the President dismissed the current scandal which has embroiled Exilium Rex Corp. as a ploy by his political opponents to tarnish the good name of the internationally renowned foundation led by King Carlos.

There was a knock on the door of the NBI Director. Michael "Mike" Lizardo, 21, one of the director's two companions inside the office got up and opened the door.

It was NBI Head Agent Basti Gomez.

"Good morning, Sir! I was told that you sent for me, Sir?"

"Yes, Basti! Come in, come in!"

Director Ricablanca picked up the remote on his desk, switched off the TV, threw back the remote on the desk, stood up from his chair, and met Basti halfway in the center of the room. The director's two companions also stood up from their seats on the cushioned sofa.

"Mike, Ally, this is Basti Gomez! You three are going to be working together in the new task force I have created!"

As Basti shook the hand of Mike and the young woman, Dra. Allende "Ally" Moran, he looked searchingly in the director's eyes for some form of hint whatsoever on what this new task force was to be about.

"Now sit down, you three!" Director Ricablanca picked up three folders on his desk and gave each of the three their respective dossiers.

As the three started to look over their respective new assignments, the director heaved a deep breath and then continued with his informal briefing.

"Now I know this is sort of a shock to you three. Mike here is just a newbie in our EDP section. While Dra. Moran has been part of our Cybercrime Division team for close to three, four years now. And, of course, I think Basti here really needs no introduction. By the way, Basti, congratulations on the latest accomplishment by your team in nabbing the 14k drug group operating in Cavite. The Mayor there has just called me up last week to send his heartfelt gratitude in helping him cleanse his city from illegal drugs, and finally putting the 14k gang out of business there!"

"Thank you, Sir! But we still have to be vigilant about the situation there! One head falls, another then rises. It's going to be hard work. But I'm up for the job, Sir!"

Dra. Moran rose from her seat on the other side of the sofa and sat beside Basti.

"Congratulations, Basti!"

"Thanks, Doctora!"

"Just call me, Ally! I didn't realize how handsome our NBI hero is in person!"

Mike almost choked upon hearing Dra. Moran fawning over Basti in the presence of Director Ricablanca.

"Well, Doctora, since you three will be part of the task force that will be operating directly under my office, I highly suggest that you three clear out your schedules and your desks ASAP because I will be doing the formal briefing next week."

Suddenly, without even knocking on the door, Atty. Renato Lagarto, a co-terminous appointee of the former NBI Director before the current director's term, bursted into Ricablanca's office.

"Ricablanca!" Atty. Lagarto slammed his fists hard on the director's desk, his eyes red and fiery with an inexplicable rage. "Why are you being so personal with me?"

NBI Director Ricablanca stood his ground and looked at Lagarto without flinching his eyes.

The assistant director was hell-bent on continuing with his tirade in the presence of the three.

"I swear, Ricablanca! If you have any plans against my Spiyamahika program, it's going to be over my dead body! My dead body!"

Lagarto slammed the door hard on his way out.

Losing his momentum in talking with the three people who was to compose the new task force, Director Ricablanca quickly dismissed them and requested that they do the complete briefing during the scheduled formal meeting next week.

As Mike and Dra. Moran walked out of the office, Basti closed the door behind them.

"Something on your mind, Basti?"

"Well, Sir, I have to tell you something very important…"

"What about, son?"

"It's about Spiyamahika."

*

As what usually happened during Monday mornings, the walled inner garden of the church was filled with some of the local devotees of Mama Mary. There might be one or two foreigners, but for the most part, the locals were the ones who usually formed the bulk of the group that sought to see the grotto in the garden.

Father Roberto had been busy the whole morning hearing confessions. Around the hour before 12 noon, he decided to give himself some time to rest. Carrying a handy pocket bible, he walked the aisles of the church where some of its patrons, mostly the senior citizens of Pantalan, took advantage of the opportunity of "talking with the Lord" outside of the formal ritual of the Eucharist.

As the good priest climbed the steps left of the altar and onto his study room, he noticed a vague shadow running past the tabernacle and then behind the blind corner of the altar where there was a votive stand for those who would want to light a candle and say a prayer for their departed loved one.

There was only one lit candle on the votive stand when Father Roberto reached the corner. The sunlight that went through the mosaic of the church window nearby did its best to illuminate the corner, but the shadows somehow made the place a bit darker than the other parts and corners of the cathedral.

As the good priest dismissed what he saw as a figment of his imagination and turned his back to go inside his study room, he heard a young man's feeble cry hiding from behind the votive stand.

"Father… please… help…"

Succubus Mode Unlocked

"From infancy on, we are all spies; the shame is not this but that the secrets to be discovered are so paltry and few."

- John Updike

*

Sefiro did not waste any time at all in giving Isabela the rundown on her being a sorceress. The realm of the Black Mirror had been aware of the fact that their existence was revealed to Isabela's world through a set of circumstances that might be deemed as fated to happen, no matter how unlikely the details might appear to humans. To Sefiro, and his kind, gods and goddesses were as real as the air humans breathe everyday. Particularly the air that the young apprentice sorceress before him was taking in: the spiritus lucis. The breath of light.

"Your people have always pictured us so differently. But, Isabela, you yourself know now that we are as real as humans. We have our own flesh and blood. But since we exist in the supernatural, we are able to do things that humans possibly cannot."

Isabela sat on one side of her bed and nodded her head.

After the minor deity's explanation to his mortal trainee, he felt that it was time to turn it up a notch when it came to the young woman's training.

"We, in the real of the Black Mirror, know more of you than you know yourself."

The young woman raised an eyebrow and let the man-god's words sink first into her brain.

"Ah, okay, okay. What do you mean by that exactly, Sefiro?"

The minor deity started pacing the floor. He was only wearing a flimsy black robe; and even though Isabela was a few feet away from him, the young woman could smell the scent of mesmerizing perfume which seemed to be naturally produced by Sefiro's flawless skin.

"In order to understand, I must show you what it means to be one of us. Look, Isabela!"

Sefiro disrobed himself in front of the young woman.

Isabela's lower jaw almost fell on the floor.

"What did you do, Sefiro? I mean... uh,,, wow..."

"Come over here, Isabela."

As if hypnotized by the sight of the well-chiseled, muscular body of Sefiro, the young woman stood up from the bed and walked over to where the minor deity was.

"You must learn to shed all your inhibitions as a human, my young trainee. A true sorceress understands that even the human act called sex is not all about sex. It is about power."

Isabela tried hard to focus her attention on what Sefiro had been trying to teach her. But apparently the sight of a naked man, maybe almost a decade older than her, was enough to trigger something in her. Something that was part of the changes she had been undergoing from girlhood to womanhood.

"Say it, Isabela: sex is power."

"Ah, sex is, ah, power."

"Why, Isabela?" Sefiro finally asked.

"Are you distracted by this?" The minor deity held the head of his well-hung cock in his hand.

"Well, uh, I have to confess to you, Sefiro, I, uh..."

"You are a virgin. We know, Isabela."

The young apprentice sorceress blushed.

"Well, if you must know, I did once..."

"Played with yourself after watching some bold videos on Father Roberto's laptop... We know, Isabela, we know."

"Wait, wait, wait! If you know everything about, then how come you never did anything to help me become more aware quicker than the regular teenage girl?"

"We need you to affirm your acceptance of your throne, Isabela. To claim for yourself as being the Queen of the Black Mirror. Now, Isabela, there's no more time to waste. It's your turn. Take off your clothes!"

*

It was almost 3 in the afternoon when Father Roberto returned home. He knocked on the door of Isabela's room once, twice, three times; but there was no answer.

Nanay Leni heard the priest knock from inside her room and decided to go outside and check.

"She's been there since this morning, Roberto, uh, I mean, Father. She received a big box earlier from LBC."

"A big box?" The good priest was a bit surprised. Again, he tried to knock on the door.

Before his knuckles could touch the wood of the door, however, it opened.

"Hi, Pa! Just got home from church? Pa, I received a gift from my classmate!" Isabela was adjusting her skirt as she explained to her father about the box delivered to her earlier.

"So what is it? Come with me, Nay, let's look!" The two followed Isabela inside her room.

The young woman had already pulled the curtains aside and switched on the light inside the room. She also placed the half-body black mirror on her night stand.

"What is it?" Father Roberto and Nanay Leni asked almost in unison.

"It's a black mirror!"

"What is it for?" The good priest asked.

"Well, you see, Pa…," Isabela was trying hard to make up a convincing lie about the black mirror, that transformed as Sefiro whenever it was required by circumstances. "My classmate is the son of a military official. He told me this was a gift from a tribe in the southern district. It is supposed to bring long life and happiness to whoever received it."

"Long life, eh?" Nanay Leni sarcastically said. "It seems its own life was cut in half before it could produce the desired results it intended for its receiver. I mean, look, Isabela, Father, the mirror's obviously broken in half."

"But, Nay, it's supposed to be broken. My classmate said that the tribe kept half of the black mirror as a symbol of sharing the promise of a long life and happiness. In short, the gift is for the long life and happiness of both the sender and the receiver of the gift."

After finishing her long-winded explanation, Father Roberto took one more stern look at the mirror, then turned around to leave Isabela's room without saying any word at all. Nanay Leni looked knowingly at Isabela. The priest's manang friday felt that Father Roberto disapproved of the gift delivered to the young woman.

Whether it was because the priest knew more than Isabela thought her father knew, or whether it was because Isabela pretended to not know more than she thought her father knew, secrets were about to be unlocked soon enough for both of them.

Number one on Isabela's list, of course, was other than unlocking herself as the supreme succubus of the supernatural world of the Black Mirror.

Daughter, Behold Thy Father

"Teach your children well / Their father's hell did slowly go by.."

- Crosby, Stills, Nash & Young

*

It was Father Roberto's turn to go inside his bedroom in their home in Baragatan. So many things. So many things were running in his head for the moment. It could not have come at a worse time. The good priest was on the verge of facing the most formidable challenge of his life: fatherhood.

As he sat on one side of his bed deep in thought, a knock came on his door.

"Enter."

It was Leni.

"Huy," Father Roberto's manang friday gestured, "why did you leave without speaking to her? What's the matter, Roberto? Not feeling well?"

"No. It's not that. I just, well.. To tell you honestly, I don't know…"

Leni locked the door behind her and sat beside Roberto on the bed.

"Len, I feel so… so guilty… It's like I've been so selfish…," Judging from the sound of the priest's voice, it was as if he was currently the one on the other side of the confessional box of the church of Pantalan. "I mean, dear Lord, I always saw myself clear when it came to most things. A man on the mission. A man of the cloth. A man for the people. But now… I never felt so irresponsible in all my life…"

"Huy! What are you saying?" Leni mildly shook Roberto's arm.

It might have been the burden of keeping the secrets of the Shafts of Light for almost five decades, it probably might have been it all along which made the priest vulnerable to Leni's sensual improprieties; but

Roberto realized that he made his own choices in life with one eye constantly on the mission.

When Isabela came into his life, Roberto still had doubts about what his Tatay Levi and Lolo Vito had placed squarely on his shoulders as a heir of the Masirikampu. More than a test of faith, it was a matter of his family's name.

Leni felt the silence of the priest beside her deafening.

"You know, Roberto, one way or another, we are all responsible for her. But we have to face it. The girl is now a young woman. And nothing in this world could change that fact anymore."

Roberto thought to himself: "Yes, nothing in this world. But outside of this world…"

"So," Leni continued on with what she thought would help the priest sort things out when it came to things related to the man's adopted daughter, "actually, this is not the time to delve into sadness or frustration. A few days from now, you will take your daughter's hand and lead her to a new life that she alone would be shaping as a young woman. Sure, we both went at her from opposite ends. You know what the people are saying about us when it came to Isabela, right? Me being the disciplinarian instilling fear in her, and you the disciple instilling faith in her. Some even say we're the perfect parents for Isabela! So perfect that we should get married to formalize our being parents!"

Roberto almost fell from the side of the bed.

"I was just kidding, Roberto! Lighten up!"

Roberto inhaled deeply. Then he looked at Leni's eyes.

"Len, I have to tell you something. About Isabela. And about that black mirror in her room."

"No, Roberto, you don't have to explain. I already know."

"You already know—?"

"Yes, yes, yes. That you want to know who's the guy who gave that stupid gift. That you don't know how to tell Isabela that you hate it.

And you're thinking of ways right now on how to get rid of that darned black mirror, right?"

"Well, not exactly what I had in mind…" Roberto decided to keep mum on revealing his secrets to Leni.

"Oh, I also know what's bothering you for so long…"

"Well…"

"Don't worry, Roberto, your secret's safe with me. You don't have to tell Isabela about us if you don't want to, okay?"

"Ah, well, Len…"

"I love you, Roberto."

Leni gently pressed her hand on Roberto's knee

"I would never do anything to jeopardize our happiness."

The two gazed at each other's eyes and understood that the time for conversation had ended.

The time for more than conversation had just begun.

"Behold thy father, Isabela." The ghost of Sefiro as the fragmented black mirror whispered on Isabela's ear.

A confusion of feelings started beating through the young woman's heart as she watched on the magical mirror how Father Roberto and Nanay Leni kept their secret all this time from her.

*

Isabela seemed on the verge of pulling out her long hair from her scalp in utter disbelief. Amidst the magical transformation as a black mirror of the nude deity Sefiro before her, she fought to change the subject immediately. To get back in the moment of what Sefiro did earlier.

"Sefiro, what were you doing earlier?!"

"I just took off my clothes, my dear child. It's all part of your training as a sorceress."

"But I thought you were a deity in the form of a man! Why would you do that in front of me?!"

"Ah, my dear Isabela. You see, while I may appear to be a man, I have no gender and no sexual inclination towards you. I am simply here to teach you the ways of the sorceress spy."

"Well, that's a relief," the young woman feigned one. "I was starting to think you had some strange intentions towards me."

"Child, you have much to learn about the world of sorcery. Trust me when I say that my only intention is to train you to be the best sorceress you can be. Our Queen of Darkness in the Black Mirror kingdom!"

"Alright, I guess I can trust you on that. But please, keep your clothes on next time. It's a bit distracting."

"As you wish, Isabela." Sefiro magically put his clothes back on with a blink of an eye. "Now, let's get back to your training. By the way, soon you must tell your father that you have found the necklace already."

Tenebris Manus

"Confusion now hath made his masterpiece."

- William Shakespeare, Macbeth

*

Inside the locked and unlit bedroom on the second storey of the chapel. A restless shadow curled on the bed. His wound shallow, but his unease deep as the darkness that swathed him like the blackness of blood seared by the heat.

Ka Iboy managed to flee from the soldiers who were tracking him. When Father Roberto found him hiding behind the votive stand near the altar of the church, the priest understood why the rebel leader was there. Sanctuary.

He kept his wound a secret from the priest. Thus, Father Roberto left him with food and clothes before the priest returned to his Calle Baragatan residence. But the wound had been infected: both the physical and the mental.

In this state of anxiety, Ka Iboy started to tak to himself.

"Alone and wounded in this dark room, I face the bitter truth of my fate. I, who once led my brothers and sisters in the fight for freedom and justice, am now a hunted outlaw, a fugitive from the very people I sought to liberate.

And yet, even in this moment of despair, I cannot regret the choices I have made. I have followed my conscience and my heart, and I have never wavered in my belief that our cause is just and righteous.

But now, as I lie here, feeling the life slowly ebbing from my body, I wonder if my sacrifice will mean anything. Will my death be a spark that ignites the flame of revolution, or will it be just another forgotten footnote in the long, bloody history of oppression and struggle?

I do not know. All I can do is cling to my faith and hope that, somehow, my suffering will not have been in vain.

O Lord, grant me the strength to endure this ordeal with dignity and courage. And grant me the wisdom to know what is right, even in the face of overwhelming odds.

For I am but a mortal man, a rebel and a sinner, but I am also a son of this land, and I will not be broken by the forces of tyranny and injustice.

So let it be written, so let it be done."

*

Mangbubuhok realized there were some things not yet fully in his hands. The occult leader of the criminal syndicate Black Moon was trying to find his way in the workings of the brain of his two targets: Isabela and Father Roberto.

Mangbubuhok, however, was not sure if the two were tipped off, somehow, by a still unknown adversary who delivered the fragmented black mirror to Isabela earlier.

Would Father Roberto be able to put things together and discover the plot to kill him and his daughter before it was too late?

Nonetheless, the nefarious head of Black Moon surmised that in the case of any assassination attempt, his two targets would focus on the preparations that the would-be assassins would be making, and the precautions that Isabela and Father Roberto were taking to try to protect themselves. Mangbubuhok was also considering incorporating elements of surprise or deception, such as a traitor within their inner circle, or a hidden weapon that an assassin could use to try to gain the upper hand and accomplish the deed.

*

At a gigantic height 6'6", Sergei, the half-Russian, half-Filipino right-hand hitman of Mangbubuhok made his entrance to the secret meeting place somewhere in Mtero Manila.

With a keen sense of urgency, Sergei met with Mangbubuhok because he told his boss he had information about the plans of the rebel forces to rescue their leader, Ka Iboy, inside the church of Pantalan, on Saturday, the day of Isabela's 18th birthday. Sergei told Mangbubuhok that they could use this information to make Ka Iboy the scapegoat for their assassination attempt on Isabela and Father Roberto.

Sergei arrived at the secluded meeting place, a small cabin, deep in the inner city of Metro Manila as instructed. He knew that Mangbubuhok was not to be trifled with, and he had come prepared for anything.

As he entered the cabin, he was greeted by the sight of Mangbubuhok, seated at a large wooden table. The occult leader's eyes glinted with malice as he regarded Sergei.

"Sergei," Mangbubuhok said, his voice low and menacing. "I trust you have come with the information I requested."

Sergei nodded, pulling out a folder from his briefcase. "Yes, sir. I have information on the rebel forces' plans to rescue their leader, Ka Iboy, from the church of Pantalan on Saturday."

Mangbubuhok raised an eyebrow. "Saturday, you say? That is the day of Isabela's 18th birthday celebration, is it not?"

Sergei nodded. "Yes, sir. That is correct."

Mangbubuhok leaned back in his chair, a wicked smile spreading across his face. "Well, well, well. It seems we have a golden opportunity on our hands. We can use this information to make Ka Iboy the scapegoat for our assassination attempt on Isabela and Father Roberto."

Sergei grinned, his cold eyes gleaming with excitement at the prospect of causing chaos and destruction. "Yes, sir. It would be a perfect plan. The rebels would be blamed for the attack, and we could continue to operate in secret."

Mangbubuhok nodded, satisfied. "Excellent. I will make the necessary arrangements. But remember, Sergei, if you fail, the consequences will be dire."

Sergei shuddered at the thought, but he knew that he had no choice but to succeed. "Don't worry, sir. I will not fail. I will make sure the plan is executed to perfection."

Mangbubuhok grinned wickedly. "Good. Then let us begin our preparations. It is time to bring chaos and destruction to the church of Pantalan."

*

Back in the gazebo of the otherwordly kingdom of the Black Mirror, the goddess of darkness, Paula, was giving last-minute instructions to Sefiro.

"So, Sefiro, do not interfere with Mangbubuhok's plans. Let them be played out."

"But, my goddess… Isabela's your…"

"Just do as I have instructed, Sefiro. My own plans can only come to fruition by hitting two birds with one stone. The first stone would be Father Roberto, together with his Shafts of Light and Spiyamahika connections. The second would be the bayok himself, Mangbubuhok, who has been a thorn at my side ever since!"

Happy Birthday, Isabela

"It takes a long time to become young."

- Pablo Picasso

*

Isabela Manlavi's 18th birthday finally arrived. But the weather was not as expected by one and all in and outside the town of Pantalan.

Nonetheless, Isabela woke up to the sound of happy birthday being sung by her foster father, Father Roberto, and her foster mother, Nanay Leni. The young woman groggily smiled and sat up in her bed, rubbing off some of the sleep from her eyes.

"Happy birthday, Isabela!" Father Roberto said, coming into her room with a tray of special breakfast for her. "We have a special day planned for you today."

Isabela thanked them and took the tray, eagerly digging into the longsilog, or longganiza, fried rice, and egg. She could not believe she was already 18 years old. It felt just like yesterday that she was an apparently scared and lost little creature taken in by the good priest and the female caretaker of the church.

After breakfast, Isabela got dressed and went outside to the living room. Once there, she was surprised to see a home-baked birthday cake and a small pile of gifts.

"Surprise!" Nanay Leni said, with a broad grin on her chubby cheeks. "We wanted to make this day extra special for you."

Isabela could not believe her eyes. This was more than she could have ever hoped for. She thanked her parents and excitedly started to open her gifts.

There were clothes, books, and even a new phone from Father Roberto. Isabela was overwhelmed with gratitude and happiness.

"I can't thank you enough for everything you've done for me," Isabela said, as tears of joy began rolling from her eyes.

*

At first, as Saturday slowly dawned, the residents of Pantalan were greeted by clear blue skies and warm sunshine. It would have been the perfect day for Isabela Manlavi's 18th birthday celebration, and everyone would have been in high spirits.

But as the morning wore on, dark storm clouds began to gather on the horizon. The sky grew darker and darker, and a strong wind began to blow, whipping through the town and causing trees to sway and leaves to scatter.

It would be reasonable to think that Isabela and her friends and family would try to ignore the storm, and would be determined to have a good time despite the weather. But as the afternoon wore on, it became clear that the storm was not going to let up.

The wind grew stronger and the rain began to fall in earnest, drenching the guests and ruining the decorations. Isabela and her loved ones huddled under the tents and umbrellas they set up in the backyard of their Baragatan residence, trying to keep dry, but it looked more and more like a losing battle.

But, as the famous quote went, the show must go on.

Though, at one point, the party set at 4 in the afternoon temporarily came to an abrupt end as the storm raged on, forcing everyone to take shelter indoors. Isabela was disappointed, but she knew that there was nothing to be done. The storm was out of their control, and all they could do was wait for it to pass.

After an hour before the Angelus fell, however, the storm finally began to subside, and the residents of Pantalan were able to emerge from their homes and assess the damage. The town was a mess, with fallen trees and debris scattered everywhere.

Despite the destruction, the people of Pantalan were resilient. They worked together to clean up the town, and Isabela's 18th birthday celebration was eventually continued for later that evening. The storm may have disrupted their plans, but it couldn't dampen their spirits.

*

It had to be noted that, earlier in the day, Father Roberto and Isabela had their heart-to-heart talk as father and daughter.

"Isabela, we have to be careful. Especially bow that you've reached the age of 18. The age which was indicated in the Masirikampu prophecies about the chosen one. If anyone finds out about our powers, we could be in serious trouble."

"I know, Papa. But it's not fair that we have to hide who we are. Why can't we just tell the truth?"

Father Roberto sighed. "Because the world isn't ready to accept us, my dear. There are those who would seek to use our powers for their own gain, or who would fear us and try to harm us. We must protect ourselves and each other, no matter the cost."

"But how can we keep this secret forever?" Isabela asked her father with an air of frustration. "It's not like we can just pretend to be normal."

"We'll have to be very careful, and always be on guard. We must never let our guard down, even around those we trust. And if anyone does discover our secret, we must be prepared to do whatever it takes to protect ourselves."

"I'm scared, Papa. What if we're found out po?"

"We must have faith, Isabela. We have each other, and we have our powers. As long as we stay strong and stay together, we will weather any storm that comes our way."

*

Neither storm nor sin would stop Nanay Leni in dressing up Isabela Manlavi with the wardrobe the woman had given as a gift to the young lady she had reared ever since she was a baby left on the limestone steps of the old chapel.

Nanay Leni undestood that the perfect dress for a daughter on her 18th birthday in the town of Pantalan, on an island in northern

Palawan, Philippines, would depend on a variety of factors, including the daughter's personal style and preferences, the theme of the celebration, and the weather and location. A few weeks earlier, she imagined that some potential options for a dress for this occasion could include the staples.

First, a traditional Filipino baro't saya, which was a long-sleeved blouse and long skirt ensemble that was often worn for formal occasions. This dress could be made of a vibrant and colorful fabric, and could be adorned with intricate embroidery or beadwork.

Secondly, a modern and elegant evening gown, which could be a floor-length dress with a fitted bodice and flowing skirt. This dress could be made of a shimmering and luxurious fabric, such as silk or satin, and could be embellished with sequins, beads, or other decorative details.

Third and last, a casual and playful sundress, which could be a knee-length dress made of a lightweight and breathable fabric, such as cotton or linen. This dress could have a fun and colorful print, and could be paired with sandals or wedges for a comfortable and stylish look.

Overall, the perfect dress for a Filipino daughter on her 18th birthday would be a dress that reflected her personal style and tastes, and that was appropriate for the theme and location of the celebration. It would be a dress that would make her feel confident and beautiful, and that would allow her to celebrate this important milestone in her life.

With her succubus mode unlocked by the gay deity, Sefiro, Isabela Manlavi chose the third option.

Perplexions

"I have seen so many storms in my life. Most storms have caught me by surprise, so I had to learn very quickly to look further and understand that I am not capable of controlling the weather, to exercise the art of patience and to respect the fury of nature."

- Paulo Coelho

*

One of the biggest surprises of the day was Basti's arrival on Isabela's 18th birthday celebration, despite the stormy weather.

Isabela had been secretly hoping for and had been eagerly awaiting the arrival of Basti, the nephew of her foster father Father Roberto. She had heard so much about Basti from Father Roberto, and was excited to finally meet him.

On the day of her 18th birthday celebration, Basti arrived from Manila during the small window that morning when the skies were still clear. Isabela was overjoyed to see him, and the two of them embraced warmly.

Both of them experiences a certain tingling sensation in their respective bodies, but both managed to control this strange sensation.

"Isabela, it's so wonderful to finally meet you," Basti said, smiling, though drenched to the teeth with rainwater. "Father Roberto has told me so much about you. Happy birthday!" The NBI head agent quickly took off his raincoat and handed a gift-wrapped box which contained the special magical instruments he and Father Roberto talked about in a zoom meeting a week ago.

"Thank you, Basti," Isabela replied. "I'm so glad you could come. It's like having a sibling here with me."

Basti nodded. "Yes, it's almost like we're siblings, even though we're not related by blood. But Father Roberto has always considered us family, and that's what counts."

Isabela smiled. "I completely agree. So, tell me, what brings you back to Pantalan? Don't tell me you came all the way here just for my birthday! I would kiss you right now if you tell me that that's your only reason! Really—are you here on vacation, or is there something else?"

Basti hesitated for a moment before answering. "Well, to be honest, I'm actually also here on official business. I'm an NBI head agent, and I've been sent to investigate a case here in our hometown."

Isabela's eyes widened in surprise. "An NBI head agent? That's incredible! I never would have guessed."

Basti chuckled. "It's not as glamorous as it sounds, believe me. But it's definitely rewarding work, and I'm glad I can use my skills to help others."

Isabela nodded, admiring Basti's dedication to his job. "I'm sure you're great at what you do. I'm sure you'll be able to solve your case quickly and successfully."

Basti smiled. "Thank you, Isabela. That means a lot coming from you. And don't worry, I'll be sure to keep you updated on the case, and we can work together to help Father Roberto and the others here in Pantalan."

Isabela beamed with pride and excitement at the prospect of working alongside Basti on a real-life NBI case. She knew that this would be a life-changing experience, and she couldn't wait to see what the future held for her and Basti.

As per his official assignment, Basti was assigned the case of the mysterious death of a young woman which appeared to be linked to the Black Moon criminal syndicate.

Claire Montalban.

*

The highly-anticipated time arrived. The blowing of the birthday candles by the birthday girl. All the party lights in the backyard of their Baragatan residence were switched off.

Isabela Manlavi inhaled deeply, and as the debutante blew out the candles on her 18th birthday, the sound of breaking glass and gunfire filled the air. The guests at the Baragatan residence screamed and ducked for cover as a masked assassin burst into the yard, a gun in his hand. The anonymous assailant then shouted at the top of his lungs, "Mabuhay ang pakikibaka para sa kalayaan ng mga anak ng bayan! Long live the struggle for our people's freedom!"

"Isabela, run!" Father Roberto shouted as he pushed her away from the gunman's line of fire.

But the assassin was faster. He fired a shot at the old priest, hitting him in the chest. Isabela watched in horror as Father Roberto fell to the ground, blood pooling around him.

She tried to run, but the assassin was on her heels. She stumbled and fell, the killer's weapon pointed at the temple of her head. She closed her eyes, waiting for the shot that would inevitably end her life.

Then, by instinct, she touched the pendant of her necklace. The Spiritus Lucis Deo. God's Breath of Light. She inhaled once deeply and then held her breath.

She waited for the shot, but it never came. Instead, she heard a loud thud and the sound of someone falling to the sodden soil beside her. When she finally opened her eyes, Isabela saw her killer lying motionless on the ground, a odd-looking knife embedded in his back.

Standing over the assassin was a mysterious figure in black, his face hidden by a hood. He reached out a hand to help Isabela to her feet.

"Come with me," the figure said in a deep, gravelly voice. "I am here to protect you."

But before the young woman could gather her senses again, the figure disappeared just as it appeared right before her eyes.

Suddenly she heard Basti's voice. "Isabela, are you alright?" She felt the man's hand stroking her hair at the back of her head. She did not see, however, that Basti's hand was bloodied all over because of him stabbing seconds earlier the would-be killer of the young Pantalan apprentice sorceress.

*

Two shadows were conversing inside the dimly-lit office of the head of the secret NBI facility, Spiyamahika, behind an unassuming kegelkarst.

"And we were invited to that birthday party. Wow! This.. this changes everything, Sim…"

The doctor leaned back on his chair to hide his countenance from the already dim light of the lamp on his office desk.

"Atty. Magalona, ever since we, me and Father Roberto, started the program 15 years ago, we both understood the kind of danger we could be faced with. Yes, you may be correct. This changes everything—to someone who doesn't a clue on what he or she in for."

Épilogue Temporaire

"When you reach the end of what you should know, you will be at the beginning of what you should sense."

- Kahlil Gibrán

*

Isabela and Basti stood in silence as they watched Father Roberto's casket being lowered into the ground. Tears streamed down Isabela's face as she remembered the kind and loving foster father who had raised her since she was a baby. Basti stood by her side, his face solemn and grim.

As the burial ceremony came to an end, Basti turned to Isabela and spoke in a low voice. "Isabela, there's something I need to tell you. Something that Father Roberto entrusted to me before he died."

Isabela looked up at Basti, her eyes full of curiosity and concern. "What is it, Basti?"

Basti hesitated for a moment before answering. "Father Roberto and I were members of a secret group called the Shafts of Light. We were created to fight against the Black Moon criminal syndicate, which has been wreaking havoc in the Philippines for many years."

Isabela's eyes widened in shock. "The Black Moon criminal syndicate? I've heard of them, but I never knew Father Roberto was involved in fighting them."

Basti nodded. "Father Roberto was a brave and selfless man, Isabela. He dedicated his life to fighting against evil and protecting the innocent. And now, it's up to us to continue his work and make sure that the Black Moon is brought to justice."

Isabela felt a surge of determination and pride. "I'll do whatever it takes, Basti. I want to help you and Father Roberto in any way I can."

Basti smiled, his eyes shining with appreciation. "I knew you would, Isabela. And that's why Father Roberto left you this." He reached into his pocket and pulled out a sealed envelope. "This is a letter that Father Roberto instructed me to open only after his death. Beforehand, he told me that it contains a map of a tunnel under the church of Pantalan. The letter indicates that the tunnel will lead us to the secret of the necklace you're wearing."

Isabela touched the necklace that hung around her neck. To the young woman, it was a highly sentimental piece of a memory she would always hold inside her heart; but she had always felt that there was something enigmatically special about it. "The secret of the Spiritus Lucis Deo, or God's Breath of Light," she whispered.

Basti nodded. "Exactly. Father Roberto believed that the necklace holds the key to defeating the Black Moon once and for all. And now, it's up to us to follow the map and uncover the secret that it holds."

Isabela took a deep breath, her heart racing with excitement and anticipation. "Then let's do it, Basti. Let's follow the map and discover the secret of the necklace. Together, we can bring down the Black Moon and protect the people of the Philippines." Though, at the back of the young apprentice sorceress's mind, she was having a few vengeful ideas to avenge her father, and even her best friend, both slain by still unknown killers in an unfortunately short period of time.

Basti smiled, his eyes shining with determination. "Yes, Isabela. Together, we can do anything. Let's go and uncover the secret of the Spiritus Lucis Deo."

About the Author

Manuel Ortega Abis

Manuel Ortega Abis, or Nonoy, refers to himself as an old-school and anonymous Filipino poet. His official website is at *https://manuelabis.com/*.

www.ingramcontent.com/pod-product-compliance
Lightning Source LLC
LaVergne TN
LVHW041551070526
838199LV00046B/1910